DRAGON WHISPERS

SIX TALES OF DRAGON ADVENTURE AND LORE

CHARITY TAHMASEB

COLLINS MARK BOOKS

COPYRIGHT

CONTENTS

Here be dragons ... six of them.

Dragons—often mercurial, preternaturally perceptive, always inscrutable.

Dragon Whispers is an offshoot of The (Love) Stories for 2020 project. In late 2019, I conceived of a project where I'd post a story on my blog each Friday for an entire year. I figured that since we were heading into an election year here in the US, we could all use a little compassion, kindness, and love.

Then 2020 actually happened.

But that's another story for another author's note.

However, during this project, I discovered I had

dragon stories—in my head and on my hard drive —enough to create their own compilation.

And it's always wise to give the dragons what they want.

As these stories are (or will be) part of The (Love) Stories for 2020 project (https:// writingwrongs.blog/2020love/), I invite you to read them for free on my blog. Barring unforeseen circumstances, the stories will remain there indefinitely (which is why I'm placing this author's note at the front of the book rather than the end).

Oh, and I lied. I have one more story for this collection, a drabble (a story exactly 100 words long) first published in *Spirit's Tincture*.

Happy reading, and let the adventure begin!

THE BARGAIN

Mirabella stood tethered to the pole, throat clogged with sulfur. The cavern yawned before her.

Behind her, villagers crouched, trembling with anticipation.

The yearly bargain was underway.

A roar. Earth-shattering footfalls. Talons scraped the earth. The dragon closed its wings about the pole; a stream of fire sent the villagers scampering.

In their wake, Mirabelle sighed.

A single talon sliced the ropes. She pulled a key from her bodice, worked it into the shackle around the dragon's ankle. He bowed his head, in agreement, in gratitude.

She straddled his neck, clutched him tight, and together they rose into the air.

ALEAG THE GREAT

The hue and cry of the villagers woke Aleag from a sound sleep. Dreams of ice and granite shattered, leaving him with the scent of spring in his nostrils—the elusive and tantalizing hint of violet, the heavy perfume of lily of the valley. He stretched, dug his claws into the earth, and peered down the mountain.

The villagers clambered up the mountainside, pitchforks and handcrafted spears clutched in their fists—as if such things could pierce his scales.

Did they need to do this every spring? At best, it was tedious. At worst?

At worse, something—or more likely someone —would knock the delicate balance between human and dragon off-kilter. Aleag was growing weary of the whole charade. He wouldn't be responsible for the resulting destruction.

At the center of the crowd, a young woman stumbled. Her wrists were bound, her feet bare and oddly pink. Her gown fluttered around her ankles like sea foam. Every few steps, she glanced over her shoulder as if the threat was behind her instead of straight ahead.

Curious, Aleag emerged from his cave, tail casting a graceful arc once free of its confines. Sun glinted off his scales, its heat warming his blood and clearing the last of the icy dreams from his head.

He could taste his next meal in the air.

The villagers approached, scrambling over the last rocks and boulders to reach the outcropping that held his cave. The lord mayor took the lead. The man's blood trembled in his veins. Aleag could feel it from where he waited.

Interesting how some men conquered fear with the threat of shame.

Then again, when you were offering up such a tasty morsel, courage had little to do with it.

Aleag deigned to meet them at the stake, the location where—year after year—they secured their sacrificial lamb, where—year after year—they would barter.

Aleag always bartered.

After all, he saw no reason to make this easy for them.

SOMEONE YANKED THE ROPE. Lily stumbled forward, more a dog on a leash than a human being. That someone jerked again. Not Peter. No, never Peter, not in his new role as village lord mayor. Peter wouldn't soil his hands in all this.

The rope passed from villager to villager—her friends, her neighbors, her patients—until, at last, it was Jack who had the unlucky chore of tying her to the stake.

"I'm sorry, Lily," he whispered, an anxious glance in Peter's direction.

"No more than I am."

She'd known from the start that if it ever came to something like this, Jack would choose Peter over her. He always had, always did, and always with an apology.

At least tethered to the stake, she could see her little cottage in the valley below. Still intact. Still safe. Someday, it might prove useful again, if not to her, then someone very much like her.

The dragon approached, footfalls shaking the ground, pebbles scattering down the slope. A few bounced and came to rest against her bare feet, the feeling of them cool against her skin, like a balm. For the first time in a week, her feet stopped their ceaseless ache.

The dragon snuffled and sniffed, the force of his exhales ruffling her hair.

"And you are?" His voice was impossibly low, a quiet murmur meant for her ears only.

"Lily." She managed that single word with her own quiet power, surprising herself, if not him.

"Of the valley?"

"If that's what you wish."

He snuffled again. "I thought I'd detected spring in the air, but I doubt my wishes have anything to do with this proceeding."

"Then we have that in common."

He surveyed her with his large yellow eyes, her startled reflection staring back at her from the dark pupil. It was an astonishing thing to be seen so completely. At that moment, Lily felt her entire being exposed—the secrets she kept in the cottage, the ones buried deep in her heart.

"And you are?" She knew his name; all the villagers did. Every spring, they scaled the mountain. Or rather, most of them did. Lily always remained in her cottage out of protest.

Until this spring, anyway.

Still, it only seemed polite to ask.

The dragon inclined his head. "Aleag."

Peter stepped onto a nearby boulder, out of grasping range, Lily noted. He wore a sky blue sash of silk about his waist, indicating his rank as lord mayor. He puffed up his chest and began to speak.

"Aleag the Great! As is our tradition, we bring you an offering of spring!"

"Are you really?" Lily asked under her breath.

A hint of steam rose from the dragon's nostrils, almost in question. "Am I what?"

"Great."

The dragon snorted a stream of fire that sent the villagers scampering down the incline. Even Peter tripped and fell backward, Jack's outstretched arms breaking his fall.

"It would seem," Aleag said, humor and heat in his words, "that I'm at least adequate."

When one was staring down certain death, one generally didn't laugh. And yet. Lily found herself biting back the smile. "What would you need to do to be great?"

"Oh, the usual, I suppose. Crush a few villages beneath my claws, lay waste to the harvest, incinerate a couple of forests." A sigh rumbled in his chest, the sensation shaking the earth beneath her feet. "I find I lack the enthusiasm for such things."

Below, the villagers scrabbled back up the mountain, slower this time, their footfalls wary. Peter glared at Lily as if she were the one responsible for his undignified tumble.

Perhaps he had a point.

Lily turned to Aleag. Oh, but he was a fine creature. If not for her untimely end, she could admire him. Indeed, a creature such as this should be worshiped.

"What's going to happen?" she asked.

Aleag swiveled his head and stared at her with the force of both eyes. Even without the stake and rope, Lily would've been trapped by his gaze alone—prey to his predator.

"My child," he said. "Have you no idea?"

PETER CLAWED his way up the boulder a second

time. Sweat had sprouted along his spine the moment they'd left the village. Now it coursed, a river overflowing its banks. The back of his tunic was drenched, the stain spreading into the sash's heavy silk.

Leave it to Lily to make the creature laugh. Laugh! Of all things.

He brushed his hands against his thighs. His wrists ached from the fall, and the tender flesh of his palms—it had been several seasons since he'd worked the harvest—stung. He pulled himself up straight. He was the lord mayor, after all. As such, he was due a certain amount of respect.

"Aleag the Great!" Peter tried for the second time. "As is our tradition, we bring you an offering of spring!"

The dragon scrutinized him, from the top of his head to the bottom of his leather-clad feet. The gaze was unrelenting. Tingling erupted along Peter's skin, a shower of needles, the sensation both sharp and tantalizing.

This is what these creatures did, of course. They made you crave the pain and welcome your own demise. Peter shook his head, blew out a breath, and cleared his thoughts.

Or tried to.

"An offering." The words rumbled as if the dragon were bored. "What if I don't find it ... adequate?"

Before Peter could answer, Lily and this ... this ... this *creature* exchanged glances. It was as if they both found the situation humorous.

Heat rose in his cheeks. "She is our most treasured asset, our village healer. We do this to honor you."

"Your healer?" The dragon swiveled his head, that remorseless gaze sweeping over Peter before the creature set its sights on Lily. "Pray tell, why would you sacrifice your healer?"

"To honor you." Peter puffed out his chest again. He knew, of course, how dragons were, how they wouldn't accept a sacrifice without some bartering, without knowing what it cost the village. The last lord mayor had told him such. That the most difficult part of the job was selecting a maiden each spring.

Truth be told? This year, it hadn't been that hard.

"So, when the blacksmith blisters his hand," Aleag intoned, "the carpenter tumbles from a cottage roof, countless women labor to birth children, are you telling me your healer won't be missed?"

"There are other healers in this land."

"Perhaps there are, and perhaps seeing how cavalierly you treat your own, they will decide not to make your village their home."

"Perhaps, but our village is filled with a number of wise women. We will do without."

His words sounded tinny, their echo doubling back on him. Behind him, the disgruntled murmur of a dozen of those wise women made his ears burn. Doubt churned in his stomach. He pressed a hand against his belly to steady himself.

Truly, Lily wasn't that skilled. Truly! Any old fool could coax women through labor and set a broken bone. Yes, Lily had the touch. The mere brush of her fingertips could cool a fever or soothe a colicky infant.

She had brought him back from the brink, certainly. Peter exhaled as if the thickness in his lungs remained. Yes, she'd brought him back; for that, he'd always be grateful. But he could not abide—

"I refused his offer."

Lily's words rang clear, loud enough—he swore —to be heard in the valley below.

"Hm?" Aleag's murmur emerged with a puff of smoke. "What was that, my dear?"

"He proposed," Lily said. "I refused. Then he threatened me, and I refused again."

"And now, you're here." Aleag swung his head around, that penetrating gaze finding Peter once again. "How interesting."

AND HERE ALEAG thought this proceeding was going to be a bore. He peered into the crowd. The lord mayor looked, in turns, a putrid, sickly green and flushed to the point of violence. Yes, shame made a man do many things he might later regret.

"We were friends, always had been, since we were children." Lily twisted, her gaze going from the lord mayor and then to Aleag. "But I had no wish to marry him. I have no wish to marry at all."

Aleag snorted another stream of smoke. "You are wise beyond your years, my dear."

Laughter rippled through the crowd. Women near the back bent their heads together, their whispers low and conspiratorial.

"Perhaps," Aleag began, and now he addressed those beyond the lord mayor and the few men who remained at his side with pitchforks and spears. "Perhaps you should rethink your sacrifice. It seems to me that a man who could be so vindictive is perhaps not the man you want as lord mayor."

Oh, and now the lord mayor turned a delightful shade of gray. He wobbled in his stance. Shame. Ambition. These things were never good for the soul.

"Stop it."

Aleag blinked. Lily's voice halted the soliloquy he'd been brewing in the back of his mind. Indeed, there was so much to work with. The defiant damsel, the spurned lover, the innocuous and yet sly third who hovered in the background. A fierce column of women who looked on the verge of toppling the lord mayor. The men, slowly but certainly slinking down the slope.

"Excuse me, my dear?"

"I said, stop it. Stop toying with us. It's deliberately cruel, and you know it."

He stared at her, his gaze unflinching. To her credit, she withstood it. "What is it, then, do you suggest I do?"

She tilted her chin in his direction and held up her bound wrists. "Take your sacrifice."

SILENCE SETTLED on the crowd before a ghastly cry went up. The sound was filled with despair and remorse, and so much shame that it shook Lily to her core.

Peter leaped forward, hands scrambling on the smooth surface of the incline. He pawed his way forward, boots skidding against the rock.

"No!" he cried. "No!"

Lily spun away from him, her whole being intent on the dragon. "Do it. Do it now."

Aleag gave her a slow blink as if he didn't need to move, as if time wasn't of the essence.

"Because it will serve him right?" he asked.

"Because every other outcome is worse."

Worse for Jack, for Peter, certainly for the village. Even if they couldn't see it.

"Let me be the last sacrifice this village needs to make."

Something sparked in Aleag's expression, a glint in those yellow eyes. His lip curled, revealing the teeth that would soon be the end of her.

And yet, Lily felt … nothing.

No, that was hardly true. Her heartbeat thrummed in her throat, the roar of blood in her ears. She stole one last glance at her little cottage below. It had been a good home. Certainly, until a week ago, it had been a good life as well.

"This is what you want?" the dragon asked.

"It is."

"Very well, then. I'm more than happy to oblige. You are the smaller morsel, but dare I say, bound to be the tastier one."

"He with the most teeth gets to say what he wants."

Aleag snorted yet another stream of smoke. "You have a sharp wit, my dear. Pity I have to eat you."

"I don't think you're capable of pity."

Those were Lily's last words. For a moment, she saw the world around her in all its colors—the glorious blue sky, the sun painting clouds on the horizon pink, the green and red-roofed cottages in the village below.

And then everything was black.

PETER FELL TO HIS KNEES. He was late, much too late. The sweat that coursed down his spine washed across his entire body, his skin flashing cold, then hot, and cold yet again. He mouthed words, senseless things, the only coherent syllable that of an ending chant.

"No, no, no, no."

The men holding pitchforks let them clatter to the ground. They crept away with barely a glance backward.

The women of the village cast him looks so caustic that certainly his skin would erupt in blisters. They, too, departed down the mountainside, in groups of twos and threes, their murmurs rising upward, taunting him.

Murderer ... coward.
Fool.

It was this last that rankled most, although Peter couldn't say why.

Then, only the three of them remained on the mountaintop: Peter, Jack, and of course, the dragon.

"Was ... was she really the last?" Where he found the courage to ask, Peter couldn't say. His words came out thick and phlegmy. He sounded like a child with a cold, not the lord mayor of a thriving village.

"Indeed. In all the years I have bargained with your village, it's a wonder no one else ever thought to ask."

Peter pushed to his feet. He wobbled, only to have Jack steady him by the elbows. He shook off his friend and stumbled forward.

"Are you telling me that all we had to do was *ask*?"

"Why not? It seems like a reasonable request, does it not? *Please stop eating our maidens, if you would, dragon, sir.*" Aleag said this last in a singsong, the taunt grating at Peter's insides.

Peter glanced around, wondering if he might pick up a pitchfork and run this damnable creature through the heart.

"I wouldn't try if I were you," Aleag said as if reading his thoughts. "The request would still have required a sacrifice. The previous lord mayor knew as much."

Peter's mouth fell open. The air in his lungs grew thin, and his breath came in gasps like he'd never inhale fully and completely again.

"Go," the dragon ordered. "Leave now. Take this knowledge and become a better leader of your village than he was."

The creature retreated to his cave. A mist

covered the cavern's opening and settled on Peter's face like morning dew.

He continued to stand there for a very long time.

At last, Jack plucked his elbow. "She's gone."

Peter nodded, his gaze fixed on the cave. He took one long, last shuddering breath and let Jack lead him down the mountainside.

THE AFTERMATH WAS Aleag's favorite part. On this side of the mountain, nothing impeded his view— no village, no smoke, no pitchforks—nothing but the endless valley and the river below. He'd take a season—spend time counting the wildflowers in all the nooks and crannies—before deciding where to settle next.

He let his chin rest on his crossed forepaws and waited.

It would be a while before the damsel in distress woke from her slumber.

WHAT LILY NOTICED FIRST, she couldn't say. The

sun warming her limbs? The cool stone beneath her back? Or was it the elusive, tantalizing scent of violets washed with fresh pine?

When she opened her eyes, nothing but the dragon filled her view. Sunlight glinted off his scales, and she squinted, raised a hand to her brow until her eyes adjusted.

She was ... alive?

"How did you sleep, my dear?" Aleag lifted his head just enough to look at her full on and then settled back down, almost like a hound at the hearth.

She raised herself on one elbow. "What did you do?"

"How did you sleep?" he asked again, not impatient, but certainly implacable.

Lily pushed strands of hair from her cheeks. She sat up and considered how she felt. Refreshed. Renewed. "Very well, actually."

"I thought as much. A good sign, that."

"Is it?"

"Indeed. The maidens who sleep the best find the most success on the other side."

Lily glanced about. Yes, she recognized this side of the mountain. Often she'd trek here, searching out herbs and rare mushrooms, gathering up the profusion of wildflowers that grew in the valleys. "Wait ... other maidens?"

"My dear, you don't think I actually eat any of you, do you?" A shudder ran through his form, scales rippling like water. "Credit me with a bit of taste."

"Then what do you do with them?"

"Chat for a bit and then send them on their way."

"On their way ... then the sacrifice?"

"Is never returning to the village, never letting anyone know they're alive. Most agree that's a small price, considering the alternative."

"So each spring, they simply walk away?"

"As you will do, as well."

Lily wrapped her arms around her legs and let her chin rest on her knees. "You agreed never to take another."

"The time had come. I was growing bored with the whole charade."

"What will you do?"

"Find a new spot to settle, another mountain. I assure you, the world is filled with mountains, with any number of well-appointed caves."

Lily stood, stretched. Excitement thrummed in her veins. No, she couldn't return to her cottage—

that was clear—but perhaps she could begin a new life elsewhere. She glanced down at her feet, the skin still aglow with pink from their scalding. Before she went anywhere, she'd need to find some shoes.

"My dear, are you willing to make another exchange?" Aleag nodded at her feet.

"I might be," she said.

"In that case, do you see that clump of violets over there, in the outcropping?"

They were a lovely bunch, lavender and cream-colored, their scent subtle and sweet. Lily nodded.

"Bring them to me?" The dragon kneaded the ground with his claws. "I don't possess the dexterity for such matters."

She gathered the bunch and then continued from there until her arms overflowed with blossoms. She returned to the outcropping and placed them gently in front of Aleag.

He plucked one and then another with tongue and lips, movements precise and dainty. He shut his eyes, and a sigh escaped him, the sound of it pure contentment.

"Thank you, my dear." He caught her in his gaze and nodded at her feet. "How did you come by such a burn?"

"When I ... refused Peter—"

"The lord mayor?"

"Yes, when I refused him, he got upset, knocked my cauldron from the hearth. The stew soaked my shoes." Lily stepped close and raised the hem of her dress. "I'm lucky it was only a bad scalding."

Aleag blew a stream of smoke across her skin. It was cool like spring, and fresh. It stole the last of the heat from the burn, the pink fading, the scars healing. Now she shut her eyes in pure contentment.

"Thank you."

"It was my pleasure. I don't often partake in such a feast." Aleag flexed his claws. "I can't pick them myself, after all."

The sound of scrabbling caught Lily up short. The noise came from behind her. She spun in time to see Jack scale the lip of the outcropping.

Jack took a few stumbling steps forward and halted. He unslung a knapsack from his shoulders and placed it at Lily's feet.

"It's not much," he said, "but there's some clothes, good boots, and a few of your books. I hope I chose the right ones, and, of course, your stash of coins from beneath the loose floorboard."

Lily shook her head. "I ... don't understand."

"Usually, my grandmother is the one who does this." Jack peered around her to address Aleag. "I hope you don't mind, sir."

"Under the circumstances? Quite understandable."

"The women in the village? They *know*?" Really? Then why hadn't she known?

"Only a few, and I only found out ... after everything with Peter."

Lily took the knapsack and ducked behind a boulder. She emerged dressed and ready for travel.

"Will you come with me?" she asked Jack.

"As far as the crossroads."

So like Jack, choosing Peter over her. He always had, always did, always would.

"He needs me," Jack said. "You don't."

Yes, perhaps that had always been true.

Lily approached Aleag and placed a kiss against his scaly snout. "You're a bastard, you know that?"

"Most dragons are, my dear."

"But thank you."

"Again, the pleasure was all mine."

Jack walked with Lily as far as the crossroads. She memorized the feel of his sturdiness next to her, his calloused palm next to her own. She'd miss him.

Even after everything.

THE VILLAGE PROSPERED under Peter's reign. The harvest never failed. The forests provided a never-ending supply of game. Every spring, violets covered the mountainside in a blanket of lavender and cream.

The sight always made him think of Lily.

As the years passed into decades, Peter became known as Dragon's Bane. He never confirmed the rumors—that he had singlehandedly dispatched a dragon from their village.

He never denied them either.

After his third wife died, Peter relinquished his role as lord mayor. He and Jack found a cottage on the outskirts of the village where they tended a few acres of land and spent long evenings in front of the hearth.

It was only then that Jack told Peter the rest of the story.

A KNIGHT IN THE ROYAL ARMS

The lobby of the Royal Arms Hotel is so very quiet, and I can taste the hunt in the air. Not that I'd planned on hunting. I only stepped inside out of the rain. Still, the thought tempts me. I don't know what sort of shadow creature lives in this space, but considering the marble floors and gilt-edged mirrors, the prize might be worth the effort.

The glimmer has lulled the concierge to sleep. He slumps over his desk, snores rattling loose paper. The doorman has sunk to the floor. With the sun about to set, that leaves me, the creature, and possibly another tracker as the only ones awake. I take a few steps further in, boots skidding against the marble, not fully committing to the hunt. Not yet.

There *must* be another tracker. Someone must have a claim on this space, and I know I shouldn't venture any farther. But there's no denying DNA, and the shadow creature that resides here is calling to me. So I blow a goodnight kiss to the concierge and find the stairs.

IN THE THIRD FLOOR HALLWAY, I breathe in dust, fingertips investigating the textured wallpaper. I remain silent and try to gauge whether that creaking floorboard gave me away.

Something always gives me away—a floorboard, the squeaking soles of my boots, a rather clumsy entrance that involves breaking glass. That's all fine when I'm prepared to hunt. Tonight I only wanted a peek.

Behind me, something rasps, brief and brisk, like sandpaper against skin. Mist fills the far end of the corridor, swallowing the glow from the sconces. I squint, but the shadow creature hasn't reached its full, solid form. For this, I am grateful. I race, carving a zigzag path along the corridor. I rattle one doorknob, then another, all of them locked.

At this point, the creature is still mostly vapor. You could poke your fingers through it. But then, you can poke your fingers through a thundercloud. That doesn't make the lightening less deadly.

I sprint down the hall, intent on the last door. I try the knob, then spin, my back against the textured wallpaper. No stairs, not even a fire exit. That's got to be a code violation. At the end of the hall, strands of gray mist probe tentatively. Something that resembles a claw solidifies and holds its shape long enough to tear a hole in the carpet.

Frantic, I try the door one last time. Three things happen. The creature surges forward, filling the hallway with its girth, the door flies open, and I tumble inside. I kick the door shut, my boots and the creature simultaneously slamming against the wood. The door frame shakes but stays put.

The room is dark, curtains drawn. My own ragged breathing fills the space, as does someone else's. I'm staggering to my feet when the lights blaze on. I flinch, cover my eyes with one hand, and attempt to protect myself with the other.

"What the hell?" a voice says.

And then I know: I'm really in trouble.

I grope for a chair and whirl it so it becomes both a shield and a weapon.

"I was here first," the voice says. The tone is strong, authoritative, but a hint of fear invades the arrogance. We all carry that in our voice, those of us who hunt. You can't touch the shadows without them touching you.

"Says who?" I counter. True, I hadn't planned on hunting tonight. Now that I'm here? Why let the opportunity slip by?

"Luke Milner," he says. "Tracker number 127."

"I know who you are." Or at least *what* he is. There are so few of us that we know each other by reputation, if not by name and face.

"I've been tracking this creature for weeks," he says. "It's on record, claim 5867. Feel free to check."

"Oh, I will." I roll my eyes.

"Plus, you totally fell in here." He shakes his head. "You don't even know your way around."

I grip the chair harder. "Oh, sure," I say. "I fell in here. I also flushed out the creature. In what? Less than an hour? How long have you been tracking it again?" I make my voice go all sweet, which is perfectly awful of me. But I can't help it. I dislike most other trackers. Like I said before, it's in my DNA. As a damsel in distress, I have good reason not to like or trust nearly everyone.

"Know the way back out?" Here, Luke Milner offers up a perfectly awful grin, providing me with yet another reason for my aversion.

While logic dictates that if you can find your way in, you can certainly find your way back out again, shadow creatures have a way of erasing that sort of logic. I do have a knack for flushing them out—and an annoying knack for getting stuck in various labyrinths for days. Normally I don't go in without a plan and a week's worth of supplies. The hotel room is covered with that same velvet wallpaper as the hall, all fleurs-de-lis and scrollwork, which makes the space feel elegant despite the freeze-dried meals and canned goods that line the dresser. Luke even has an adorable little camp stove. Plus that queen-size bed? Big enough for two. Not a bad setup, and I can't help but be a little impressed.

He waves his hands as if he can halt both my gaze and my thoughts. "Oh, no. Don't even think about it. My claim. My creature."

"Which you can't seem to flush," I remind him.

The trashcan overflows with wrappers and bottles. A room service tray holds a pot of coffee and pitcher of cream. One whiff tells me it's starting to turn. He's been here for a while without any luck. It's hard to catch a shadow creature on your own; it's even harder to trust another tracker. He can't leave the hotel without risking a claim jumper. But why stay if you can't draw out the creature to begin with?

"You saw it then?" he asks.

"Claws. Sharp. Not sure what it is, but it's big." I shrug. "Maybe a dragon."

He pauses as if considering this—and me. "What makes you so special, then?"

It's a fair if somewhat passive-aggressive question. "I come from a long line of damsels in distress."

Luke snorts.

"Shall I step into the hall and demonstrate?" I gesture toward the door. All hunts require bait. Usually, that's me. I survey the room again. This Luke Milner doesn't seem to have anything that resembles bait.

"You don't look like a damsel in distress."

True. I keep my feet in boots. You try running around in satin slippers or high heels. Tulle and lace and all the rest? Highly flammable, especially in the case of dragons.

"It's in the blood," I say. "Did I not fall in here exactly when I needed to?"

"I was opening the door."

"See? You must have some latent knight-in-shining-armor blood running through your veins."

Luke makes a face.

Okay, *very* latent. But it's there. He's too well-stocked and prepared to be anything else. In theory, I should like that in anyone. Plus, he has that knight-in-shining-armor *look*, wavy hair and features chiseled in all the right places. His eyes might glint with humor if he weren't so surly. Something tells me Luke Milner is often surly.

I've never had any luck with knights in shining armor. They're always too little, too late, and I always end up bound ankle and wrist, eyebrows singed.

Luke narrows his eyes to slits. I cross my arms over my chest, prepared to wait him out. He glances away, but in the mirror, I catch his reflection—all sour milk and resignation.

"Do you have a name?" he says at last, "or do they just call you CJ?"

"C ... J?"

His smirk provides the answer. CJ. *Claim Jumper.*

"I'm Posey Trombelle," I say, putting some teeth into my name. "Tracker number 278."

"Posey?" He makes another face.

"It's short for Poinsettia. I was a Christmas baby."

His expression goes blank. When he doesn't respond, I add, "My sister was born in February, on the fourteenth. Trust me, she got it worse."

"Well, what do you suggest we do ... Posey?"

"What were you about to do when I fell into your room?"

"Go out," he says. "Reconnaissance."

I raise an eyebrow. Because that? Fairly obvious.

Luke rubs his hands across his face. A growl begins in his throat, but the sound is all frustration without any bite. "I have a theory," he says, "that there's more treasure to be had by not slaying the creature —

"Because most of it is in the lair," I finish.

Oh, of course! How clever. Once you slay the creature, access to any treasure in its lair vanishes. I can't help it. I like the way he thinks. Maybe this Luke has more knight in him than his sour-milk expression suggests.

"You figure out how to do that," I tell him, "and they'll have to call you Sir Luke."

LUKE STARES at the document on the coffee table, pen clutched in his hand.

"You can't do this without me," I point out.

His knuckles go white.

Granted, a handwritten agreement on hotel stationery pales when compared to a notarized contract. Under the circumstances?

"In fact," I say, tapping three paragraphs down on the paper, "you can't get a better deal than this."

No one would intentionally draw a creature to them, but I've signed on to do just that. Of course, I'm uniquely suited for the task. But while Luke searches out the lair, I must fend off the creature. While I often find myself in precarious situations, I seldom walk into them of my own volition. At least not while leaving myself wide open for betrayal. I occupy the creature, and he runs off with the treasure. I try not to think about that scenario too much.

At last his grip loosens on the pen. He scrawls

his name across the bottom of the page, nearly obliterating my own.

Next comes a grappling hook and some rope, which Luke secures at my waist. He threads a whistle onto a length of nylon cord. He ties the ends and then places the whistle around my neck.

"Last resort," he says. "If you need me—"

"Just blow?"

He cringes. An angry flush covers his cheeks. Before he can turn away, I touch his arm. "Hang on."

From the depths of my cargo pants pocket, I pull a bandana. "A knight shouldn't venture out without a token," I say and tie it around his arm. As tokens go, one-hundred-percent cotton is no substitute for silk, lace, and embroidery. However, the bandana *is* pink.

"Seriously?" Luke eyes the bandana. His fingers twitch over the knot like he might undo the whole thing and toss it on the floor. Instead, he presses his palm against his jeans and sighs.

"See if it doesn't bring you luck," I say.

"I don't believe in luck."

"You should." I give him a two-finger salute and slip out the door.

I TAKE soft steps down the hallway, retracing my original path. I even zigzag, fingertips brushing the textured wallpaper on one side of the corridor and then the next. The ventilation system breathes to life, its steady, mechanical hum the only other sound.

At the corner, I pause. Things are too empty, too quiet. The space around me feels thin, like something else is using up all the available oxygen. Something large. The elevator lobby is the perfect place for an ambush. At least, it's where I'd set one up.

The marble floors in front of the elevator sport a faux Persian rug, a Queen Anne side table, and chairs upholstered in the most amazing shade of canary yellow. The space is pristine. I sniff the air. No lingering scent of sulfur, no rot. What about some slime, a tuft of fur, or even a scale on the floor? Nothing? I taste the air one last time, not trusting this good fortune, but my feet are already moving. To hesitate is to lose this chance.

I rush to the elevators, push the up and down buttons, then retreat to the safety of the stairs.

No sensible tracker uses the elevator—not if

they can help it. It's the equivalent of stepping into a lunchbox. Still, it's a handy ruse. A damsel in distress inside an elevator? There's no better bait.

The elevator bell chimes. The doors whoosh open. Dark mist spills out, and a roar echoes against the walls, the sound hearty. The creature must be on the verge of transforming into something solid—and deadly. I'm half a step inside the stairwell when mist curls around the handrail and engulfs my fingers. I glance at the gleaming claws clicking against the lobby floor, then behind me to the creature forming on the stairs.

Here be dragons. Not one, but two. And here I am, right between them.

I cast my gaze upward, searching for a handhold, a window or vent to crawl through ... or that chandelier.

The elevator doors start to close, then spring open again. The creatures are solid enough to trigger elevator doors, not to mention claw, bite, and chomp. They are certainly solid enough to do a damsel-in-distress grab-and-dash.

You know, the usual.

With a hand on the grappling hook, I squint at the chandelier. Will it come crashing down on me mid-swing, effectively doing all the bone-crushing work for the dragons? Steam fills the elevator lobby area. The dragons won't risk a full blast and burn themselves out of their playground. But a stream of fire in my direction?

I don't wait to find out. I swing the grappling hook up and over the chandelier's arms. Light bulbs shatter. I tug. Cracks appear along the ceiling. Plaster dust floats down, fogging the air and coating the floor, the table, the dragon. Before I can swing, a great sucking comes from the elevator —a wind tunnel drawing me in. I grip the rope and brace my feet against the floor. Then the winds reverse.

The explosion of sound startles me. No heat. No fire. Just slime.

"Gesundheit," I say and swing up and over the sniffling dragon.

I land in the hallway, carpet soaking up the sound of my boots. Iridescent dragon snot speckles the textured wallpaper and coats the toes of my boots. I yank the rope one last time. The entire chandelier and half the ceiling crash to the floor. I sprint around the corner to avoid ricocheting debris. Even so, I choke on dust. My eyes water. I blink fast and hard, taste the grit against my lips. At the end of the hallway, a door flies open.

Luke sticks his head out. "What the hell?"

I give him a little finger wave and run.

ONLY UNDERWATER LAMPS light the pool area, bathing everything in a liquid blue. My boots squish against damp tile. Moist air clings to my face, turning the plaster dust into muck. With my back to the wall, I ease the lifesaving pole from its bracket. Since Luke's grappling hook is now part of the third-floor decor, I need *something*—a tool, a weapon. I test its weight against my palm. Light but strong. It will do.

Now that I'm here, I have the thankless job of luring both dragons to this spot. That shouldn't be too hard. After all, I'm a damsel in distress. Luring is what I do. I take mincing steps around the pool and coo stupid things like, "Oh, no, I might get my satin slippers all wet."

I've never met a creature yet who could tell the difference between satin slippers and steel-toed boots.

Minutes tick by with nothing but the gentle lap of water and my damp footfalls. This was the plan. We didn't have a backup plan in case the creatures didn't show. I'm a damsel in distress. They *always* show.

Except for now.

I kneel at the pool's edge and rinse the plaster from my face. Perhaps it's the water's chemical cocktail—too much bleach and chlorine—that convinces me, but nothing supernatural ever happens in this particular space.

But if the creatures didn't follow me (and they should have, they really should have—I should be trussed up now, tied to the diving board or cooking in the hot tub), then there's only one other spot they could be: their lair.

Which is where Luke was headed—without any backup plan of his own. Can I intercept him? I glance at my watch. Plenty of time before sunrise. Still enough time to—possibly—save Luke. Without another thought, I sprint past the heated towel rack and lounge chairs and crash into the glass doors separating the pool from the mezzanine.

I push. I pull. I rattle the handles so hard the glass shudders. Then I see a telltale glint on the other side of the doors. A dragon scale. I whirl and face the pool. What will it be? Damsel-in-Distress

Stew? Or perhaps Luke is the main course, and I'm dessert.

Panic and chlorine clog my throat. Another way out—there must be one. I slip across damp tiles, careen into the changing room doors. These, too, are locked. I survey the space—the lounge chairs, discarded drink glasses with pink sludge and crushed paper umbrellas, a stack of rumpled towels—and discover a way out.

I find the service elevator behind a screen. Steam hisses and clouds roll through the room, as if the water in the pool is already boiling. I wonder if the dragons plan to serve me *al dente*. As soon as the doors screech open, I jump inside, press every button I can, and realize I'm still clutching the lifesaving pole only when the doors clang shut.

I LAND in the most obvious spot for a lair, down in the basement. The dank and dark, home to boilers and furnaces and the creatures most everyone else has forgotten. Only in this case, it seems the creatures have forgotten this space. Then again, these are dragons—by their very nature, quirky and particular. In this case, there's a pair. A couple, perhaps?

Oh. A couple. Of course. I push the up button on the elevator. There's no time for stairs. I can only hope I'm right and don't end up as a char-broiled snack. When the doors open, I step inside and select the modern equivalent of the high tower: the penthouse suite.

You'd think, as a damsel in distress, I'd be well acquainted with penthouse suites. Sadly, my luck runs toward trolls and ogres. On the rare occasions I'm captured, I end up in landfills or junkyards or, for the occasional eco-conscious goblins, recycling centers.

The doors open on the penthouse level. Smoke fills the elevator compartment. The acrid scent tickles the back of my throat, and I choke on a cough. I step out and crunch something beneath the sole of my boot. The remains shine in rainbow patterns the way only a dragon scale can.

I take a cautious look around. The glimmer is in full force here. Despite the smoke, I can taste the magic that lets the dragons lie dormant during the day and come out to play at night. They haven't taken over the entire floor, not yet, but the lair is well established.

I creep forward, pole outstretched like a spear, eyes cast downward. The last thing I want is to track through a pile of ash. That can mean only one thing. The tracker community may be combative, but the death of one of our own weighs heavy. My stomach squeezes tight. I clutch the pole harder. I want to close my eyes, because I don't want to see that pile of ash. I keep them open out of fear and respect.

At the end of the hall, I brush fingertips over the penthouse door then press my palm against the paneled wood. Warm, but not searing hot. That's something. Now for a distraction. I need something loud and sure, something these dragons won't miss.

I lean against the wall, and that something thumps against my chest. Luke's whistle. I grip it between my teeth and blow with all my might. Then I sprint down the corridor and launch myself behind a settee. The hiding place is flimsy. But once dragons get up a good gallop, they have a difficult time stopping, never mind turning around.

The penthouse door flies open. Claws scrape against the Italian marble floor, leaving wide grooves in its surface. The dragons galumph straight for the elevator, bypassing the settee. I crawl from beneath it, scrabble to gain purchase, then race for the penthouse.

I slam the door. It doesn't matter if the dragons hear. They're too clever to stay fooled for long anyway. Still, I throw the deadbolt for the slight delay it will give me. For good measure, I jam the lifesaving pole behind the handle.

"Luke?" I call out.

A grunt comes from the bedroom. Among satin sheets, rose petals, and candlelight, I find him, all trussed up, bound ankle and wrist, damsel-in-distress style. He grunts again, words muffled by a pink bandana—*my* bandana—gagging his mouth. So much for luck.

I can't help it; I know it's cruel. I laugh.

"You wouldn't happen to have a knife, would you?" he says when I undo the gag, a frown fighting the relief on his face.

"Swiss Army." I slice through the ropes around his wrists and set to work on his ankles.

A crash reverberates through the entire penthouse. My hands shake and the blade skitters up and over the rope, but it only catches on Luke's jeans. A whoosh fills the air, followed by the cheerful crackle of burning wood.

"We have all of three seconds," Luke says.

In those three seconds, I hack away the last of the rope. Luke smashes the window with a chair. He secures a grappling hook (one covered with plaster dust) and swings us—me clutched in one arm—out the window, past jagged glass, and over the ledge.

We land one story below, breezing through an already-opened window. When our feet touch ground, Luke releases me. I tumble into yet another canary yellow chair, knocking it over. I suck in air free of smoke, grateful for the hard floor that has just bruised my hip bones. As landings go, this one wasn't half-bad. I catch Luke's eye and point to the window.

"I like to go in with a back-up plan," he says.

An admirable quality for a knight in shining armor.

"You're pretty handy with a knife," he adds.

"You're not bad with ropes."

The building trembles. Plaster rains down, dusting my skin—again. The elevator doors pop open and shut.

"We should leave," I say. "They'll destroy every-thing just to get to us."

Even their own playground. Threat to their

treasure brings out the nasty side of shadow creatures.

To my surprise, Luke takes my hand to help me up. He keeps a grip on it during our entire flight down the stairs. Even outside, with the first rays of sun banishing the night, he doesn't let go. He pulls us forward, intent on getting us away, while I scan the structure.

"All clear?" he asks.

"Looks that way. For now."

Four blocks from the hotel, we slow our steps. I keep the vigil, always tossing a quick glance behind. With the rising sun, the glimmer loosens its hold. The dragons will return to mist and shadows. The hotel will right itself before any of the regular guests can notice anything amiss. Already, glass in the smashed windows has repaired itself.

"I never thought to look in the penthouse until you came along," Luke says.

I inspire thoughts of the penthouse? Is this a good thing?

"The living room was the treasure trove, but I decided to check the bedroom before leaving," he continues. "I walked in on them while they were ... I mean, he was—"

"Entertaining a special lady friend?" I supply.

A flush washes across his cheekbones—a hint of pink to match the sunrise. It's kind of adorable.

"Yeah." He clears his throat. "That."

Luke pulls a small velvet sack from his shirt. "By our contract." He tips the bag and coins flow into his palm. "Fifty-fifty split. You earned it."

"So did you."

"It wasn't all bad," he says, "working with you."

Is that a compliment? I peer at him, intrigued. "Well, you *are* good with ropes," I say. "And I don't loathe you like I do most knights in shining armor."

He tosses the coins in the air and catches them neatly again. "When was the last time you earned a haul like this?"

Almost never. Damsels in distress always get the short end of things, even when we're the ones who make things happen. I can't count the number of times my fellow trackers have left me bound, wrist and ankle, and made off with the treasure. Even though my boots are singed and snot covered, my hair a plaster-streaked mess, this time, the prize was worth it. This time, I had a worthy partner.

"There's a lot more where this came from." Luke stares hard just past my shoulder, like the only way he can say this is to not look at me. "We could spend days, weeks, and still not find it all."

We? "So you're not reporting me as a claim jumper?"

His lips twitch. "Well, you know, I can't seem to flush them on my own."

"That's my specialty."

"We'd need a contract."

I nod toward a diner at the end of the block. They serve a huge breakfast special—eggs over easy, sizzling bacon, pancakes drenched in maple syrup—the perfect meal after a night of successful tracking.

"Everyone knows a contract written on the back of a paper placemat is totally binding," I say. "We could talk about it. Maybe over some coffee?"

The sun crests the hotel, casting the street in a glow to rival the canary yellow furniture, banishing the creatures to shadow for another day. We turn toward the diner. Luke tosses the coins and lets them fall into his hand one last time.

"Maybe we should," he says.

vy Bremer stood at the edge of Merryside Township, shotgun in hand. Behind her, flags from the Fourth of July celebration fluttered. Pollen hung in the air, casting everything in a yellow glow.

Her arms ached from gripping the shotgun, her hip protesting the weight of the revolver strapped there. Both weapons were heirlooms, handed down from generation to generation until they sat in the town museum, displayed in shadow boxes, their purpose forgotten. That morning, Ivy had smashed the glass and freed them both.

Mayor was a thankless job—interim mayor even more so. It served her right for skipping that last city council meeting. Or maybe not. Maybe it was because she'd been standing in this very spot twelve months earlier. She'd seen him first. Either way, she was here now.

He was coming. The breeze shifted, lifting sticky strands of hair from her neck. A buzzing filled the morning, the sound like the drone of a prop airplane. Each approaching footfall shook the earth, a reverberation that traveled up her legs, captured her limbs and wrapped around her heart.

Ivy glanced behind her, at the town too quiet to be a real town, and caught the menacing shadow of the catapult. Silver pails glinted, and hoses coiled like snakes, strategically placed for the fire brigade.

As if that could stop the burning.

When had she known? Certainly not that first day, when she'd nearly drowned in the depths of those amber eyes, his gaze alight with the heat of flame behind it. Amber eyes! Why hadn't she thought to question that?

The breeze picked up. The footfalls remained ever steady, and the buzzing seemed to penetrate her eardrums. In the fields bordering the road, cornstalks quaked. To Ivy, it looked as though they trembled with fear.

When had she known? Not at that first city

council meeting, when they unanimously voted him mayor. She'd only felt hopeful. Not when he'd taken her under his wing—how apt—a month later. She'd only felt protected. Not when he proposed. She'd only felt cherished.

Was it the record profits for every business in Merryside? The flood of scholarships for their graduating seniors, the grants to improve the schools, the roads, the infrastructure?

They'd basked in the bounty, never thinking of what it might cost.

So, when had she known?

After the warmest January on record?

Perhaps.

After surveying the charred remains of the winter wheat?

Definitely.

Now she stood at the edge of town, the only one who never took coin, the only one who gave, the only one who could stand there. She widened her stance. The shotgun, heavy as it was, reassured her. The revolver at her hip felt right, like she was born to wear it.

He would not pass.

A thin column of smoke rose from the horizon. His footfalls shook the ground so much that her knees buckled—certainly, that wasn't from fear. At first, all she saw was his head and the misty smoke issuing from his nostrils. The tip of his tail flicked into view. Had he been a dog—which, of course, he wasn't—Ivy would've said he was happy to see her.

Then all of him came into view. His bulk cast a shadow along the road, shading her from the sun long before he took his final step.

"Ivy." Her name from his mouth was both sulfurous and sensual. "Did the cowards send you to stop me?"

"I came on my own accord. I'm the mayor now."

A laugh burst forth, one filled with brimstone. "A thankless job, is it not?"

His scales glinted in the summer sun, throwing rainbows across her vision. His talons sunk into the ground rhythmically, as if he were a cat kneading its owner's lap. The claws churned up asphalt and dirt. Despite herself, Ivy calculated the repair costs and weighed them against the town's diminishing budget.

But his eyes. Those amber eyes. Those were the same. She recognized herself in their reflection.

"Do you bar me entrance?" he asked, the question issuing with a stream of smoke.

She hesitated for a mere fraction of a second. "I do."

He bowed his head as if in defeat. "Do you love me?"

This time, she spoke without the hint of a delay, her heart answering for her. "I do."

Something crackled then, like a fire coming to life. Behind her came a whisper of sand and the sound of bows being pulled taut. She held up a hand, and both sounds ceased.

"Then grant me entrance," he said, voice low, melodious, almost human. "Let me collect what's mine."

With deliberation, Ivy set the shotgun on the ground. She unbuckled the holster from around her waist and placed that next to the shotgun. She felt suddenly lighter without the weight of either, like she might step off into the air and float away.

Instead, she took a single step forward. Waves of heat washed over her skin. Her lungs struggled for oxygen, and sweat coursed down her spine.

"This is what's yours." She placed her hands on either side of his muzzle and kissed him.

The earth trembled. Ivy squeezed her eyes

shut, but that didn't stop the single tear from slipping down her cheek. In an instant, the dry heat stole it away.

The sizzling started near his tail. It traveled along his spine, the scales falling away in ones and twos, and then faster, their clatter like rain on a tin roof. Then her world imploded in a cloud of acrid smoke.

The wind picked up again, chasing away the clouds of smoke and revealing a man crumpled on the road in front of her. There he was, that same dark-haired stranger who had strolled into town a year ago.

Ivy crouched next to him, eased her thigh beneath his head, cradled his face with her hands.

His eyes locked onto hers. "Why?"

"They would've harnessed you, used you—or killed you in the attempt."

"Or I, them. That's the way it is, the way it's always been."

"Not now. Not anymore." A tear wove a track through the grime on her cheek. "I had to stop this … them, and I'm … sorry."

He shut his eyes, bliss washing across his face. He had the look of a man finally free. "I'm not."

Another teardrop slipped from her cheek and

hissed against his skin. His eyes—those amber eyes—flew open. He brought his fingertips to his mouth and then pressed them against her lips in a dry and dusty kiss.

"Goodbye, Ivy." He smiled at her. In it, she caught the feral glint of teeth and tender mouth that had so willingly kissed her own. "And thank you."

The fire that consumed him burned cold. The smoke was thick but sweet. One moment, his weight was solid against her thigh. The next, it was as light as the pollen in the air.

Then, he was gone.

All that remained was dust and ash. Something shimmered there among the specks of gray and black—a single scale. Ivy held it between her finger and thumb, turning it this way and that. Its surface shattered the light, threw a rainbow of color so bright it might blind. She let it rest in her palm before tucking the scale into her pocket.

Ivy stood. She didn't bother to strap on the holster. She simply pulled the revolver from it. A single shot incapacitated the catapult mechanism, its net hanging loose and now useless. With the shotgun on her shoulder, she marched into town.

No one said a word as she returned the

weapons to the museum. They were heirlooms, certainly, with their own sort of magic. Ivy licked the dust from her lips and regarded the relics, locked away in their shadow boxes once again. With luck, that was where they'd stay.

After that, all she had to do was point. Without a word, children collected the buckets. The volunteer fire brigade rolled up the hoses. Members of the city council dismantled the catapult, destroyed the arrows, filled in the trap.

Ivy surveyed the work. Behind her, the cornstalks whispered in the wind. On the breeze, she heard the echo of his promise.

I give you one year and one year only.

Everyone had wanted more, her heart included. She pulled the scale from her pocket, and it glinted in the sun. She held it aloft and let it cast a rainbow across the entire town of Merryside.

Everyone froze in place, like they had that first day a year ago. For a moment, her heart leaped; something that felt like hope filled her chest. Ivy glanced behind her, willing him to step into view.

What she saw instead, through that prism of light, was what could be—if they let it. That was its own sort of hope.

Ivy pocketed the scale. Decision made, she

walked toward the town hall and the mayor's office. The breeze dried the last remaining tear on her cheek.

Yes, she thought.

She'd give it a year.

DRAGON'S END

The knock on my door comes before sunrise. Three quick raps that sound sharp and official. When I answer and see Mayor Simos on my stoop, the words *sharp* and *official* sear my thoughts.

"It's time," she says.

Her face is creased from sleep and the weight of her office. A breeze rustles loose strands of her hair, wisps escaping the coronet braids.

I want to ask *time for what*, but her expression is cold and foreboding. I know I don't want the answer.

"Bring your tools," she adds, and then, almost as an afterthought, "and the book."

Ah, yes. The book. A simple word that answers all my questions.

I know where it is, of course, locked in the trunk at the foot of my bed. The key, heavy cast iron, weighs down the cord looped around my neck. The cast iron flashes cold, then hot, against my skin.

I'm not certain I remember how to insert the key into the lock, not certain I can lift the lid. I haven't done so since my grandmother passed the book to me before she passed on herself.

"Miri," the mayor prompts, and she is all sharp edges with a razor-like gaze.

"Yes, sorry. Just a minute."

I don't invite her in. Instead, I shut the door against the protest that's forming on her lips. I sag against the wood. There are few privileges to being me, but this is one of them.

The trunk at the foot of my bed is ancient and solid. The wood is reinforced with iron bands, the lock larger than both my fists. The key slips into the lock easier than I think it should. The tumblers click with far more assurance than I feel.

When I lift the lid, a fine layer of dust bursts into the air, filling my mouth, grit stinging my eyes. My nose twitches, but I hold in the sneeze.

I stare at the inside of the trunk, at the items I thought I'd never need to use. The saw with its serrated edge. The plane and the awl. The long, elegant pick with the hook at its tip. I pack these into a canvas bag. Next comes the book.

No one has touched it since my grandmother wrapped it in linen and placed it here. The trunk itself hasn't moved in decades. I now sleep in the bed she slept in, the bed she died in.

The second my fingertips brush the linen, I'm afraid the soft material will crumble in my hands. The book must remain wrapped, at least for the trip to the caves. After that? Well, after that, I guess we'll see what's inside.

I open the door on Mayor Simos, her fist poised to knock. The reprimand is sharp in her eyes until her gaze lands on the bundle in my arms.

Even Mayor Simos respects the book.

The sun casts a glow on the horizon. There's enough light to paint the sky indigo. And enough that I can see the playground where the village children gallop and run with the hatchlings, the earth bare and packed from feet, claws, and the swish and thump of tails.

When I was younger, I sat far back from the

playground, up in the tree that shades the house my grandmother—and now I—live in. With my belly flush against a thick branch, my arms wrapped tight, I'd watch, envy fizzing inside me.

I wanted a hatchling of my own. I wanted to be chosen.

I am, of course. Chosen, that is. The book in my arms is proof of that. But I would never choose this path for myself. I would never choose it for anyone else, either.

Mayor Simos leads the way. Her coat, trimmed with gold braid, sways as we trudge toward the foothills north of the village. Cottages give way to pastures until we reach the foothills. The sun crests the horizon. Its warmth touches the back of my neck, almost like it's urging me forward.

Tendrils of smoke issue from the caves. These caves, the ones closest to the village, are not our destination. This is where the hatchlings sleep. Their gentle snoring makes me think of puppies dozing by the fire. Somewhere, deep down, that envy fizzes once again.

Mayor Simos casts a glare over her shoulder as if my longing is both tangible and unseemly. I will my expression to remain placid, and we continue our trek up the mountain.

The snoring grows deeper, more sonorous the farther up we go. The cave openings are larger. If you were to wander inside, you might be lost for days—or forever. It would all depend on the humor of the occupant.

At last, we reach the final cave on this branch of the path. Dragon's End, we call it. Nothing but blackness pours from the entrance. Worse is the silence. I strain my ears, hoping for a muted snore, but hear nothing.

"How long?" I ask.

"Five days, we think," Mayor Simos says. "It's hard to tell. They don't need much in their retirement, so the shepherds seldom visit more than once a week."

I nod as if this is vital information I can use. It isn't. I have no idea what will greet me when I enter the cave.

We stand at the entrance for so long it becomes clear that Mayor Simos is waiting on something. Profound words? A dismissal? I don't know. But there is one thing I'm sure of.

I go in alone.

I turn to do just that, but the mayor takes my arm.

"Miri, I'm sorry."

"Sorry?"

"It may have been more than five days."

"Has no one come around to check?"

I see the answer in her gaze. No, no one has, perhaps not for a very long time.

Instead of envy, anger bursts to life inside me. How could no one check? You could send a child of five up the slope. It isn't dangerous. They care for our own in the way we do their hatchlings. They would never harm a child.

I clutch the book to my chest, the linen rustling in my hands.

"I'm sorry," Mayor Simos says again. "I should've sent someone around. I simply didn't think..."

I shake my head and shake away her apology. Maybe it's her fault. Maybe it isn't. I'm not sure it matters. No one in living memory has performed this task. Even my grandmother was a small girl when her own grandmother told her of the last dragon tended to in this manner. That tale has been lost over time. No one knows, for certain, what happened.

This is not supposed to be happening. I was never meant to take this trek up the path. I was supposed to live my quiet life. At some point, I'd give birth to a girl, who in time, would birth one of her own. I would pass the tools and the book onto my granddaughter. This undertaking is one that skips a generation.

Dragons live for such a long time. Chances of any of them needing our services are inestimably small. None of us ever thinks we'll be the one to journey up the mountain, enter a dark and foreboding cave, crack open the book, and read the words inside.

After that? Here's where the oral instructions become vague. My grandmother wouldn't—or perhaps *couldn't*—tell me.

I go in alone. Without Mayor Simos. Without any counsel. Without any hope of coming out again.

I draw in a breath. The sun has touched the valley below us. If I listen hard, the delicate snoring of the hatchlings fills my ears. I step forward, the cool air of the cave washing over me. Before I can dive in, before I can fully commit, Mayor Simos touches my arm.

"The book," she says.

Ah, yes. The book. I consider it now, still clutched against my chest.

"In a week," I say. "Send someone in for it. A child would be best."

Her grip on my arm tightens.

"They would never harm a child," I add. No matter what mess is left in my wake, this mountain possesses enough residual enchantment for a child to navigate into and back out of the cave. "A hatchling, perhaps, could go with them."

Her grasp lessens, but I still feel her fingers against my skin. I don't know what else she can tell me, but I want to enter the cave before she delivers any additional bad news.

So I wrench free, my arm and then sleeve slipping from her hold. I dive into the cave, committing fully. This is one rule I know, the one rule my grandmother insisted I follow.

Once past the threshold, do not hesitate.

BUT I DO. I halt several steps inside the cave. Behind me, the entrance is barely a flicker of light. Before me? The cave splits in two, no four, no six directions.

"Which do I choose?" I say these words aloud

as if there's something else in the cave with me, something sentient and far cleverer than I am.

Nothing answers my plea except for the echo of my own voice, tiny and forlorn. I peer down each tunnel, but nothing distinguishes one from the other. Perhaps they all lead to where I need to go. Perhaps that's why there's no need to hesitate.

I pick the fourth tunnel, simply because I like the number four, and stride forward. The moment I do, a rumbling sounds behind me.

Rocks tumble and slide down the sides of the cave. I dash forward, pebbles and stones chasing after me. The walls of the cave shake. The earthen floor trembles, my feet skidding on the unstable surface. At last, a final boulder fills the path and blocks the entrance completely.

Yes. Of course. Do not hesitate.

I take quick, shallow breaths in the dust-laden air. The taste of earth fills my mouth. My heart thunders, much like the rocks and stones did. I wait until the dust and my breathing settle.

I peer toward the entrance. "How will they retrieve the book now?" I'm not sure who—or what —I'm asking. The rocks that block the path? Whatever force sent them tumbling in the first place?

As if in answer, a hint of sulfur rides the air.

"I guess that's their problem, not mine."

A rumble reaches me. I want to say it sounds like a laugh or, at the very least, a snort. More likely, the rocks are merely settling.

It's not dark. At least, not as dark as it should be. A thin sliver of light emanates from the depths of the mountain. I've already hesitated enough.

I follow the only path open to me.

THE STRAP of my canvas sack bites into the flesh of my shoulder. My arms ache from clutching the book. My fingers cramp from where I've gripped the sides. I can feel the hours I've trekked in my legs. My mouth is parched.

The muted light guides me. It's barely there, this sliver of illumination. I don't question it. To question it is to lose it, and I can ill afford to lose this one small advantage.

I have no provisions, didn't think to bring any. Slowly, over the past hours, my anger at the shepherds has simmered into sympathy. How do you care for something can't find?

And if I can't find the dragon? What then?

The thought makes me stumble. I reach out a hand, my aim the cave wall, or really anything to keep me from falling, breaking an arm—or worse, a leg. The moment my fingers brush against the cave's surface, a golden glow fills the space.

I remain there, palm flush with the cave wall, the stone cool beneath my touch. The glow around me, however? That looks warm and inviting. My eyes adjust, and I step closer to inspect the source.

Embedded in the walls, the ceiling, and even the floor are coins, layer after layer of them. Gold and silver shine forth. The coin of our realm, yes, that's expected, but it's more than that. I trace my fingers along the bumps and edges, trying to discern the languages written there. They are either from places too far away or too long ago for me to recognize.

I continue forward.

Other hues join the gold and silver of the coins, the walls now studded with gems—rubies and sapphires and emeralds. Some fall as I pass, as if the slight breeze from my movements is enough to dislodge them from their perch in the cave wall.

I wonder at this. Did the shepherds never wander this deep into the cave? A single gem could keep a family fed for generations. Certainly, the dragons allow this sort of barter—a small token in exchange for care.

A wave of dizziness strikes me. The air is, perhaps, a bit thin back here. Still, it would be worth the journey, even without the lure of riches. I don't understand why no one has ventured this far into the cave. I would gladly tend to a dragon, were I to have one.

Gladly.

The dizziness crashes over me again, forcing me to my knees. Before me, the path is pristine. Behind me, my footsteps are sharp outlines in the dust. No one has been this way for ages. My chest tightens until pain radiates along my breastbone. I'm not truly dizzy. I'm not deprived of air. This is something else, something that's simmered and fizzed for a long time.

All I ever wanted was a hatchling of my own.

What I have now is someone's loyal and neglected companion, a creature who, while not dead, is not that far away from death.

Dragons can be killed, certainly. In battle. With the sharp edge of a sword angled just so or with boulders flung with catapults. But they can't die naturally, not as humans do. As part of our alliance, we offer them this one, final service.

It falls to one family, generation after generation. This family is forbidden any other contact with dragons, from hatchlings to elders. It's said to contaminate the pact. Often we're never called upon to complete this final task.

Until we are.

Like today.

I FIND MY BREATH. A few moments later, I muster the strength to stand and for the journey still ahead of me. The cave glows blood-red now from the gemstones in the walls. Perhaps this is intentional, meant as a warning, and my pulse beats in my throat.

I round a bend in the cave. And there, just like that—blocking my way forward—is a dragon. Its girth at midsection blocks my view of its tail and the cave beyond. I can only assume there's a cave beyond, at any rate. Perhaps the cave ends here, and the dragon, grown so vast in old age, can no longer crawl free.

The claws on its forelimbs shine like mother of pearl. Its eyes are closed, mouth as well. If the creature breathes, I cannot detect it. Perhaps someone—a shepherd, maybe—has already done my job.

But there is no stench of death, of decay. The cave is dry, the air scented with a strange mix of brimstone and pine. It is not unpleasant.

I ease the canvas sack from my shoulder. The tools jangle, and I freeze, afraid the noise will wake the dragon.

It doesn't move.

I place the book, still in its linen wrap, on the floor as well.

I don't know what to do. It occurs to me that the answers are in the book. That's why it's been passed down from generation to generation, cared for, but never read. I've never even been tempted before. I only ever wanted a dragon, never to kill one.

With careful fingers, I unwrap the linen. The leather cover is worn, the gold embossed title barely legible. I turn to the first page and find ...

Nothing.

I flip to another page, and then another. I tear through the book, unconcerned with its age or condition. Nothing but yellowed parchment greets me. No words, not even barely legible ones in faded ink. All the pages are blank. At last, I stand

and shake the book, hoping for a loose page or a note or something to flutter to the cave floor.

"I don't understand."

I whisper the words. They swirl in the space around me, their echo soft yet insistent before the sensation of being scrutinized washes over me.

I glance up and find myself staring into the golden eye of an ancient dragon.

EVERYTHING I THOUGHT I knew about my task has vanished. I'm to take my tools, the book. I am to perform what amounts to last rites for an ancient dragon. It will be in such a deep sleep that the steps I must perform to end its life won't disturb it. This, my grandmother assured me.

Now that ancient dragon is gazing at me. A stream of smoke rises from its nostrils. Again, that odor of brimstone and pine surrounds me. I can taste the smoke against my tongue. The book slips from my fingers and crashes to the cave floor.

"I see they've sent me a child."

The voice is deep and sonorous. It rolls through the space and shakes my bones.

"I'm no child." My voice quavers, but the words

come stronger than I expect. I lift my chin. "I live on my own," I insist, as if this is proof of my maturation.

The dragon snorts a spurt of smoke. "Little more than a hatchling."

"What am I to do?" I point to the book. "It doesn't say."

"Doesn't it? Are you quite certain?"

Oh, spare me mind games with an ancient dragon. I'm ill-equipped for this sort of sparring. Besides, it must know even if I don't. But it will no doubt make me work for that knowledge.

"Am I to kill you?" I see no reason not to be blunt.

"Are you? That seems rather rude. We've only just met, after all."

"Then am I your...?" I trail off, a wholly different thought occurring to me.

"Sacrificial lamb, the morsel meant to appease me?" It tilts its head so both glowing yellow eyes can survey me, from the top of my head to the tips of my dusty boots. "You're rather small for that."

"Then, what am I?"

Its claws retract and then rake the earthen floor in front of me. "What you are, my child, is very much stuck."

I VERY MUCH AM. Stuck, that is. Had the shepherds performed their assigned tasks, there would be provisions in here, a cistern of water at least.

"Why am I here?"

"Have you consulted your book?"

I spear it with a glare. Without water, I won't live out the week. So I will be fierce in my dealings with the dragon.

The creature snorts another laugh. "Humans, always so inquisitive, and yet, so oddly obedient. Did it never occur to you to have a peek inside? Gird your loins for your one task in life?"

Well, no, it hadn't. I spent my time gazing at the hatchlings. "I never wanted this."

"Well, it seems to me you have it." A sigh rumbles in its throat, dual streams of smoke rising from its nostrils. "A child, and an incurious one at that. What a disappointment."

"At least it's mutual."

"Oh, perhaps this child has some fire, after all."

The dragon looks not at me, but past me with so much concentration, I must resist the urge to glance over my shoulder. That's what it wants, of course. But no one shares this space with us.

"We seem to have reached an impasse," the dragon says. "You have no idea how to complete your task—"

"Do you?"

The dragon regards me with narrowed eyes before continuing. "It's any guess who will succumb first. I will be reduced to some nether-slumber while you." Once again, it surveys me from head to foot. "Will eventually shrivel up. Will I be conscious long enough to blow the dust of your bones from this spot? Who's to say? Shall we place bets? Winner take all?"

My heart thuds heavily in my chest, a slow, painful sort of beat. Perhaps this is why elder dragons are banished to the upper caves. All I ever wanted was a hatchling, a dragon of my own. But this one? It's an old, bitter, cruel thing, and I want nothing to do with it.

There's no escaping its girth, but I find an outcropping of rocks on the side farthest from the dragon. I take my tools and the book.

Yes, even the book. The leather is soft enough, and so are the pages. It will make an adequate pillow. Perhaps that's all it was ever meant to be.

"Ah, yes, and now the poor thing pouts." Its words are a mere whisper, although clearly, it wants me to hear them. "I abhor tears," the dragon adds, louder now. "So, if at all possible, refrain from crying."

This last is the only thing we agree upon.

I comply.

IN MY DREAM, I am a warrior, a dragon as my mount. In my dream, we soar through the air, dodging arrows alight with flame. In my dream, the roar of battle shakes my bones.

My eyes fly open. The roar continues even as my dream fades. The world is dark, my bed like stone, nothing but the scent of brimstone and pine.

Then I remember.

The roaring grows ever louder. In the middle of the cave, the dragon thrashes its head. Its eyes are shut tight. It must be dreaming. The same sort of dream? Of battlefields and fire? Or is this something more, something worse?

It thrashes again. The agony in its cry races up my legs, my spine, settles at the base of my skull. I don't think. I do not hesitate.

I rush forward, dodging its swinging head,

nearly eclipsed by its jaw. I've never touched a dragon before. But from my perch in the tree, I've watched the village children do this so many times.

I leap and wrap my arms around the dragon's neck. I hold on with all my strength even as my legs swing beneath me. One foot connects with the dragon's chest, although I doubt it feels the impact.

"Shh." I keep my voice low and soothing. There's a trick to this, to the hushing of dragons. To say I have no training is true. But I listened; I practiced using that same tree branch. "Shh."

Its head continues to swing, but slower now. My arms ache, but I clutch its neck, my feet scraping the cave floor.

"Evelynne … Evelynne."

The cry rips through me. I've been so consumed with wanting a dragon of my own that I never considered what happens when the human a hatchling first bonds with is killed or dies.

How many humans does a dragon lose during its lifespan?

It could make you bitter. It could make you cruel. Perhaps this is why, at a dragon's end, they are banished to the upper caves.

"Evelynne."

The dragon's swaying comes to an abrupt halt. I dangle from its neck. I cannot see its face, but I suspect those great golden eyes are now open.

I let go and drop to the cave floor.

It takes one look at me and then collapses as if its head is too heavy for its neck.

I AM A BITTER DISAPPOINTMENT. The yellow gaze the dragon casts tells me that. I remain immobile on the cave floor, palms against the dusty surface.

"You should not know how to do that," it says.

No, I shouldn't.

"Lace your hands," it commands.

So I do. True, it took years to learn the correct placement, of which finger goes where. Incorrect placement of fingers, of hands against a dragon's neck will enrage rather than soothe. It's a skill even those with hatchlings find difficult to perfect. Indeed, I had no idea if I was performing it correctly at all.

Until now.

"How do you come by this knowledge, child?" A fiery edge laces the dragon's words, and its displeasure tastes like sulfur.

"My house overlooks the village playground." My voice comes out steady and dull. "I would watch the hatchlings and the children. I would practice on a tree branch."

"There's more to it than that." The dragon shakes its enormous head, its jaw whooshing mere feet above me. "There's the bonding, the spellcasting. You should not ... we should not."

Because it's forbidden, this contact. No thrill of fear courses through me, no regret. I would gladly calm this creature once again, given half a chance. I would gladly do it even if it meant my death. To prove it, I push to stand and anchor my hands on my hips.

Those great amber eyes blink, a shuttering of its gaze. When the dragon opens its eyes once again, something has shifted in its expression.

"What have they done to you, child?"

I shake my head, uncertain what it means.

"Why sequester the most talented humans like that?" The dragon murmurs the words, the question meant for its own pondering rather than for me.

Despite that, I decide on my own question. "Why do they banish the old ones to the caves?"

The dragon swings its head around so quickly

that I'm nearly flattened against the floor. It regards me for a moment before speaking again.

"Forgive me, child."

"Whatever for?"

"My temper, my rash judgment. Undoubtedly I've lived long enough not to give in to either."

"Or maybe it's because you have lived so long you gave into both."

Something sparks in that golden gaze. Its lip curls, revealing sharp and gleaming teeth. "Yes. Precisely. Do you suppose they count on that?"

Do they? I glance back at the way I came. Even if I had strength and time on my side, digging through the debris would be impossible. I peer into the darkness behind the dragon's girth.

"What is at the other end?" I ask.

"Other than my tail?"

"Yes." I laugh because its tone is sly and full of humor. "Other than that."

"A dead end, appropriately enough."

I turn my gaze upward and follow the trajectory of the smoke that rises from the dragon's nostrils.

"That is merely a thin layer of rock," I say.

"Oh, my child, I am old."

"So old as that? Truly?"

"My wings. I—"

The walls around us groan, and the dragon trembles with the effort to spread its wings.

"You see," it adds. "I have tried."

"But, they have given me tools." I race to the alcove and weigh each tool in my palm, judging the merits of each. I return with the awl.

I hold it up so the dragon can see.

"Indeed," it intones. "That was their mistake."

The dragon lowers its head. A thousand times, I have seen the children and their hatchlings perform this maneuver. I step carefully, only lighting a foot on its forehead before settling between its horns.

Something washes over me, that scent of pine and brimstone again, along with something more —the feeling that I belong here.

The dragon raises its head, so my own nearly brushes the cave's ceiling.

"Close your eyes," I whisper.

With my first strike, dust rains down, followed by a stream of sunlight. It touches my cheeks and makes the dragon's scales glow a fiery red. Its power, its strength, rushes through me.

This is why they confine the ancient ones to Dragon's End. Or perhaps it's why we're both here.

Together, we are something more, something powerful.

With a final chip at the thin crust, the earth that blocks the way out tumbles down.

"You're free," I say.

"No, my child, *we* are." A stream of smoke rises from its nostrils, and this dragon reminds me of an old man with a pipe, contemplating a riddle. "I don't suppose you've had a flying lesson, have you?"

"I don't suppose I have."

"But you've seen how it's done."

"A thousand times."

"Then you should be adequate. But first things first. Go get the book."

The book? I peer to where it still remains on the floor, leather cracked from where my cheek rested against the cover.

"Don't you need to return it?"

The slyness in the dragon's voice has me sliding down its neck, scooping up the book, and then returning to that spot of honor.

"I have no saddle," it says, "and no reins. You'll have to hold on."

"I have years of practice."

The dragon's wings tremble and shake. Its hind

legs quiver. With a mighty leap, it clears the edge of the cave and unfurls its wings.

"What is your name, child?" The question reaches not my ears, but my mind. Its thoughts touch mine, and the sensation is as intimate as a kiss.

"Miri."

"I am Mercurial."

"Of course you are."

The dragon snorts a laugh and sends sparks into the air. "It is also my name."

Mercurial swoops toward the village, wings shadowing the earth below. We are close enough now that I can see the chaos erupt on the playground. At the sight of Mercurial, a dozen hatchlings scamper and fling themselves in the air, wings beating furiously until they tumble and land once again. Their children race after them, laughing and crying out.

Work at the mill halts. The village elders emerge from what must have been a meeting, Mayor Simos among them.

"Now, my dear."

I toss the book into the air. When it's halfway to the ground, Mercurial shoots a stream of fire at it.

The book lands at the mayor's feet, flames chewing through the parchment.

"What a shame," I say.

"Yes. All that knowledge, forever lost." Mercurial circles the village a final time. "Where to, my sweet?"

"The farthest I've ever been from home is Dragon's End."

"Then hang on. We have the entire world before us."

So I do. I entwine my arms around Mercurial's neck. I don't look back.

Not even once.

Isabelle Sterling pulled the pickup truck off the gravel road and bumped her way to the windbreak thirty feet in. With the engine off and the windows rolled all the way down, it was quiet—at last. A soft breeze whispered in the tall grasses and rattled cornstalks.

Isabelle jumped from the cab. The tallest stalks reached well beyond her waist. She peered down row after endless row, all black earth and rich green. The scent of soil was thick in the air, warm from the July sun.

Farming wasn't one of her skills. Marilyn wouldn't let her near the enclave's gardens—not even the potted herbs—for fear she might wilt them. Still, even Isabelle knew this was a good omen.

She headed for the passenger door and the precious cargo belted in the front seat—like a toddler. Her truck still wore the dust of Georgia, the black paint flecked with red, the deep rust the color of blood. She wore it too. Every time she licked her lips, she could taste the red clay earth.

Isabelle eased the wooden crate from the cooler in the front seat, kicked the door closed, and headed for the road.

The rest of the trip would be on foot. She wiggled her toes inside her combat boots. Since being discharged, she tugged them on once a year for this trek up the bluff.

They'd carried her through Afghanistan; they could carry her here as well.

At the crossroads, she inched forward, just enough to stand in the shade cast by the stop sign. Her truck waited patiently behind her.

Anyone traveling this road would disregard it, maybe figure a farmer was checking her crops. Or more likely, a farmer had abandoned it there in the windbreak, keys in the ignition, and left it and everything behind—a relic to relentless toil and debt. She'd seen three such pickups on her way to the bluffs.

Isabelle sighed. It wasn't the truck she was worried about.

This was her fifth year up the riverside bluff.

This was the year she wouldn't come back down.

She felt the rumble first through the soles of her boots. All the hairs on the back of her neck stood at attention. She spun, jumped back, heart pounding a cadence she couldn't control.

Breathe, breathe, *breathe.*

In the distance, a white pickup truck barreled forward, a cloud of dust blooming behind it—just a farmer, and nothing more.

Just a farmer.

She was, in the words of Marilyn, overreacting. Or hyper-reacting. After five years back on the soil of Black Earth, Minnesota, she knew better.

Or at least everyone thought she should.

The dust cloud grew larger, billowing like a sandstorm. Instead of slowing for the stop sign, the driver was gunning the engine and planning to run straight through.

She backed up, stumbled over the edge of the ditch.

It wasn't far enough.

The damn truck was coming straight for her.

Deliberately.

What. The. Hell.

The truck swerved, and she pitched backward into the ditch. A spray of pebbles pelted her bare arms. She lost her grip on the wooden crate. It fell to the ground with a crack, the sound like a gunshot. Its contents spilled among the rocks and weeds.

The truck flew through the stop sign. Then the driver jammed on the brakes, backed up, and came to a halt on the road right above her.

Isabelle blinked and braced her feet against the earth. The rumble of the engine competed with the roar of her pulse. Dust floated on the air, filled her mouth, scratched her eyes.

From inside the cab came the relentless hammering of death metal. The driver lowered the volume and then hung himself out the window, fingers drumming the flame decal on the side of the door.

"Sorry about that, honey. I didn't see you there."

Like hell he didn't. Isabelle gave him a stare, the one she'd perfected in boot camp, the one without a trace of emotion except for silent contempt.

"Need a ride?"

"Oh, I'm good." Her palms stung. Her tailbone ached. But what hurt the most were the remains of her cargo scattered all around her.

There was no salvaging that.

"You sure you don't need a hand?" The driver drummed the side of his truck even harder, a strange, staccato beat that made her heart pound a warning.

"Positive."

"A pretty girl like you, out here all alone? Someone might get the wrong idea."

"Someone might, but not you," she said, weaving magic into her voice. "You're smarter than that."

She could see the spell weave around the guy's head, tangling with sweaty strands of blond hair, clouding his blue eyes. And she saw the moment he shook it off, too.

Sadly, he wasn't smarter than that.

"Those peaches wouldn't be for me, would they, sweetheart?" His gaze went not to the scattered fruit but to her chest.

"No." This time, Isabelle dispensed with magic.

Instead, she infused her words with all the Georgia sugar she could muster. "But these are."

With that, she raised both her middle fingers.

It was a dumb move, but after all the searching, the bartering, and thirty-six hours of driving, she didn't need to deal with some dude-bro joyriding around the area, scaring livestock and running over cats.

He wasn't local. Local boys (and girls) knew better than to get stupid around the river bluffs. They'd head into Mankato or even drive up to the Twin Cities.

This guy? If he didn't leave now, he might not leave at all. Not today of all days.

His fingers stopped their drumming. The knuckles of his hand went tight.

She needed to end this—quick.

Isabelle bared her teeth. The glamour was simple, barely a spell at all. She preferred fox or coyote. Today she wasn't taking chances.

She went with mountain lion.

During her first year in college, after her roommate's disastrous encounter at a frat party, Isabelle had taught her the trick—along with some hand-to-hand combat moves. Despite evidence to the contrary, the enclave insisted that there were those who could weave magic—and then everybody else.

Isabelle didn't believe it. Everyone had magic. Of some kind.

Except for maybe dude-bro here.

He blanched, blinked, and gaped, his mouth open like a fish left to flop around on the dock. Without taking his eyes off her, he put the truck in gear and inched respectfully up the road. At the stop sign, he took a right, the way leading to the interstate.

"There's a good boy," she said, her voice barely above a whisper. "And don't come back."

ISABELLE USED all but one bottle of water to give the peaches a bath. She cradled each one in her palm, the way a mother might hold an infant's head. She washed away the dirt, used a fingernail to pry pebbles from the tender flesh, and placed each one back into the crate as if tucking it in for a nap.

And she still had the three-mile walk ahead of her.

"Uphill, both ways," she said—ostensibly to

the peaches—and laughed. Then she placed her palm against her heart and waited.

She wasn't sure what, exactly, she was waiting for. But the gesture calmed her, reassured her that her heart was still where it should be, that it still beat, that neither it nor she was completely broken.

A breeze chased strands of hair from her cheeks. The crossroads were quiet once again.

It was time.

She tucked the last bottle of water into a knapsack, hefted the crate to her hip, and started her trek up the river bluff.

THE BARTER HAD COME through at the last minute, as barters tended to do. Isabelle needed twelve perfect peaches. And no, she couldn't dash into a grocery store and toss a handful into a shopping basket.

Peaches, plucked by hand. And not just any hand, but that of enclave matriarch. And not just any peaches, but ones from Georgia.

Peaches were plentiful. What Isabelle lacked was something to offer in return. Then, she connected with an enclave courier in as desperate of straights as she was.

After that, it was nothing but the whisper of wheels against the interstate and some truly terrible talk radio. At last, she reached the red clay of Georgia, where her counterpart, a woman named Denisha, met her at the southern enclave's peach orchard.

"Oh, snowdrop," Denisha said when Isabelle hopped out of her truck. "Let's get you out of this heat."

Isabelle laughed. She'd been to Georgia before —three weeks of airborne school in August, no less. But that had been a lifetime ago, and her blood was sluggish and thick from Minnesota winters.

She grabbed the cooler from the seat. The thing was icy, even after all that driving. A trace of its contents filtered into the thick Georgia air, at odds with her surroundings. A harsh, cold, fishy odor that—judging by Denisha's wrinkled nose— was overwhelming the sultry, sweet scent of peaches.

Inside the orchard's office, they headed for the kitchen area. Denisha poured them both some sweet tea. She was about Isabelle's age—late twenties or so, and she wore her hair in a coil of braids on top of her head. She looked like a queen capable of ruling her own enclave.

With the first sip, the sugar flowed through Isabelle's veins. Enclave brewed. It had to be. There was enough magic mixed with the sugar and caffeine to not only revive her but fuel her drive back home.

"So this is really a thing," Denisha said while Isabelle unpacked the cooler.

"It's a thing." Isabelle held up one of the packages. "Straight from the lutefisk capitol of the world."

The dried cod, soaked in water, then lye, and then water again—because who the hell eats lye—was a gelatinous, smelly, and baffling delicacy. She'd grown up in Minnesota and didn't understand it. She had no hope of explaining it to someone out of state.

"I thought she was joking with this request." Denisha shook her head. "I'm really hoping she doesn't ask me to share this year."

Isabelle's hand stilled on the package, the cold burning her fingertips. "She shares?"

"Sometimes. Depends on the request. Honestly, I think it's partly a test, you know—*will you do my bidding* and all that. But it's worth it, right? I wouldn't give up being a courier for anything."

Oh, how Isabelle wanted to ask. She wanted to ask *so badly*. Did Denisha see their enclave's patron? Speak with her? Share the yearly offering? What was that like? The thought of it made her heart drum against her ribcage and her palms sweat.

"Yeah," Isabelle said, heat prickling her cheeks, betraying her. "I wouldn't give it up either."

Denisha collected the packages of lutefisk. "So, I cook this ... how?"

"You can boil it, but it's probably better if you bake it. And if you have any bacon or pork drippings, you can serve that on the side."

"Everything's better with bacon."

"In this case, it might just save you."

Denisha laughed. "This is going to be an adventure." She packed the lutefisk into the refrigerator and then filled a thermos with sweet tea. "For your drive back."

"You don't—"

"Oh, yes, I do. You saved my ass. Those." Denisha pointed to where a crate of peaches sat, twelve perfect ones in a bed a straw. "Are for your patron. But these?" She hefted the thermos. "And those." Denisha gestured to a canvas sack overflowing with even more peaches. "Are for your drive back. Trust me, those things are magical. You'll eat the entire bag before you get home."

Denisha walked Isabelle to her truck and then gave her a hug so heartfelt it chased the air from her lungs.

"Text me if you need any help with the lutefisk."

"Count on it."

Isabelle drove off, opting for back roads rather than fight Atlanta's rush hour traffic. She felt as if she were leaving behind a friend, although really, she'd only known Denisha through messages on the courier group chat.

What did couriers do before the internet? In the Black Earth town hall, there was a photograph of a woman—a Sterling woman, one of Isabelle's ancestors—carrying a basket of something dear cradled in her arms.

The woman's feet were bare, her dress faded and frayed. The entire town looked as though it'd been coated in dust. In the background, an ancient Model T sat, discarded, forgotten, or most likely, both.

Isabelle thought about that woman on her drive back to Minnesota, wishing she could ask whether being a courier had been worth it.

Halfway up the bluff, the urge to pluck a peach from the crate and take a giant bite nearly overwhelmed Isabelle.

Denisha had been right. If not for her own bag of peaches, Isabelle would've eaten the offering. After that, driving past Black Earth and heading straight for the boundary waters—and paddling into Canada—would've been her only option.

It was one thing to scramble for an offering at the last minute, quite another to deliberately sabotage yourself.

Oh, but the peaches were tempting. They honeyed the air. The phantom sensation of juice running down her chin, sticky and tart, had her swiping at her skin. She'd eaten the entire bag within hours, amazed they hadn't sent her racing for a rest stop bathroom.

But these were enclave peaches, picked by a matriarch. Overindulging wasn't a danger; it was mandatory.

From this point on the river bluff path, she spied the cave opening, but only because she knew where to look. It was the darkness between pine needles and leaves. It was the cool that chased away some of the day's heat, sending a wash of goose bumps across her bare arms and legs.

She reached the spot where the mosquitoes stopped nattering in her ears and biting the back of her neck. The spot where most people turned around, their legs suddenly and oddly tired, their sunburn fierce despite thick layers of sunscreen, their water bottles mysteriously empty.

Isabelle kept going.

The path turned rocky. During her first run as a courier, she'd pulled on the combat boots on a whim, more from nostalgia rather than practicality.

Turned out to be a wise decision.

Her heart pounded again. Isabelle paused, shifted the crate on her hip so she could hold it with one hand, and pressed her free palm against her chest, waiting once again.

Her heart thrummed with a steady thump, thump, thump. During her last Army physical— one for yet another deployment requiring yet another round of shots—the doctor had paused, stethoscope pressed against Isabelle's chest.

"Has anyone ever told you that you have a heart murmur?"

Isabelle's breath caught in her throat. She gave her head one slow shake.

The doctor listened, the crease between her eyebrows deepening. "Strange no one has ever … huh, this is weird. I'm going to order some tests."

The words froze Isabelle in place. She knew, even without the tests. It was the enclave.

She was being called home.

Even now, when her heart pounded or skipped a beat, when the air felt odd in her lungs, she'd hold herself still, listen with all her might, as if somehow she could hear the defects of her own heart.

She continued the trek, the climb registering in her thighs now. This last stretch always made her doubt. Was she on the right path? Would she walk in circles, searching for the cave and never finding it?

Then the entrance loomed, dark and foreboding, a place for bears or wolves or definitely something that might swallow you in a single gulp.

And well, yes, their patron could do that. But

she—like all patrons—had a particular palate. Human flesh wasn't on the menu. Isabelle adjusted the crate in her grip.

Apparently peaches were.

She stepped across the boundary where the path ended and the flat, smooth surface of the cave entrance began. Cool air washed over her, chasing the sweat from her skin. A burst of color filled her eyes. Gemstones glinted in the sun—blood reds to dazzle, blues the color of midnight, and greens that made her think of those endless fields of corn.

The gems looked ripe, like they were their own kind of fruit. You could reach out and pluck one from the wall—if you were foolish enough to try, that is.

In the center of the entrance stood a small altar made of marble, its surface only a few inches larger than the crate she carried. The first time Isabelle had placed an offering there, relief filled the breathlessness in her lungs. Certainly she'd never be asked for something she couldn't carry.

In all five years, she hadn't. Perhaps that was enough of a reward.

She crouched and brushed the marble surface and then exhaled to chase away any errant grit or dust. The altar was clean; it always was. But it felt right to do this, to make this final gesture before she left.

Assuming she would leave this year.

As always, if her patron lingered inside the cave, Isabelle couldn't detect her. No sigh filled with smoke. No tail scraping the cave floor. Nothing but the gemstones glinting playfully and the altar waiting for her offering.

She eased the crate onto the surface and stood —one step back and then another.

Nothing.

Perhaps she'd been wrong about the five years. But no, when she'd returned from the Army, Marilyn had specifically said the previous courier —Isabelle's second cousin—had "finished" with her duties.

Her matriarch hadn't elaborated on what "finished" meant, exactly, only that the woman was nowhere to be found. And that it was Isabelle's turn.

And ten years ago, before she'd enlisted in the Army, there'd been another such turnover. Indeed, it was one of the reasons she did enlist. Out of sight, out of mind.

Now, here she was. Another Sterling woman

after five years of service to a patron she'd never seen, never mind spoken to.

She'd tried, of course, that first year. She called out, peered into the cave, even dared to take a few steps inside. The hollow space swallowed her voice. The light from the gemstones faded a few feet inside the void. No scent of brimstone or smoke, only that of clean, dry earth. If her patron lingered somewhere beyond, shrouded by the dark, Isabelle couldn't tell.

If not for the vanishing offering—last year's had been Mozart Kugeln from Vienna—she'd say nothing inhabited the cave at all.

So that was it: five years and nothing. Perhaps Marilyn would meet her at the crossroads where she'd left her truck and relieve her of her duties. Maybe this was like the Army. She'd done her time, served as best she could, but lacked the ... *heart* for anything else.

But it had been a good five years. She'd gotten her degree and traveled the world—this time to places where people weren't shooting at her.

That was worth something.

"Thank you," she said into the stillness. "It's been an honor to be your courier."

Isabelle was at the boundary, toes of her

combat boots flirting with the edge, when a sonorous voice sounded behind her.

"Oh, my child, that sounds like a goodbye."

It was only after her discharge from the Army that Isabelle found herself freezing at the oddest provocations. She couldn't account for it.

After all, she'd stood in the open door of a C-130, the pines of Georgia thick beneath her as the plane banked for another run at the drop zone. She was out the door the second the light turned green, no hesitation. She could work in the sand, the mud, the rain. She knew when to be still and when to move.

But here in the civilian world? Here with her patron?

She froze.

"It's all right, my dear." The words were low, infused with brimstone and heat, mist and flowers.

It was such a strange, enticing combination that Isabelle found herself turning around. She froze once again, this time in awe. Her patron was a shimmering green that changed with the light— from one angle, the icy green of new growth, from another, the deep somber skin of a ripe avocado. Flecks of red raced along the surface of the scales. The forked tongue was red as well.

But the eyes were a glowing amber. And it was those serious eyes that surveyed her now.

"Are you really a dragon?" It was an impertinent sort of question, and Isabelle almost wished she could bite it back.

"Some people call me that. I prefer to think of myself as myself."

"Me, too."

"Indeed. It's a Sterling trait, one I've always admired."

Isabelle glanced about the cave. She knew that she wasn't some sort of damsel-in-distress sacrifice. *Why now* and *what next* both hovered on the tip of her tongue. At last, she went with:

"I don't understand."

"The enclave still needs you, my dear, they have always needed you and the Sterlings before you."

"To do what?"

"The hard work of making ends meet, I'm afraid."

"But, the gardens, and the farm, and the—"

"Etsy shop?" The dragon's voice rose, more

amused than sardonic. "Not enough to survive on, never mind thrive. We have always sent the Sterlings into the world. They've always been the most capable of handling the vagaries of life."

Like making a thirty-six-hour roundtrip for a crate of peaches or dealing with dude-bros in their pickup trucks.

"Yes, exactly that." The dragon grinned.

At least, Isabelle assumed that's what all those teeth meant. She recalled the glamour she'd used on dude-bro. Forget fox, coyote, or even mountain lion.

Maybe she'd been a dragon all along.

"Indeed," her patron said. "You've also been a soldier and a scholar. For five years, you have catered to my ... whims. You're ready to strike out on your own."

"I'm to leave the enclave?"

"Not permanently, but for the time being, yes."

"Will the enclave call me home again?"

Wisps of smoke rose from the dragon's nostrils. She shook her head as if startled by Isabelle's question.

"My child, didn't you know? That was me."

Isabelle touched fingers to the left side of her chest. "But—"

"I had to break one small part of you so that you could come home to us." The dragon paused, and it was as if she spoke the next word with great reluctance. "Intact."

The meaning of that word—*intact*—sank in immediately. Isabelle had kept herself from watching the news, from keeping up with her old unit, searching the internet for details. Somehow, she knew. She knew exactly how that last deployment had ended.

The dragon blew out a smoke ring. It broke against Isabelle's chest, soothing but not healing her heart.

"It's not all bad, a whispering heart," her patron said. "If you listen closely, it can tell you what you want."

"I'm afraid I can't hear it."

"You will. With time." The dragon inclined her head toward the peaches, still on the altar. "Now, will you stay and join me for this repast?"

Isabelle took two steps forward and knelt at the altar. "I will."

A FULL MOON helped Isabelle navigate the path

down the river bluff. Once in her truck, she rested her arms on the steering wheel and gazed through the windshield. Above her, through the fringe of cottonwood leaves, a field of stars littered the night sky.

She was going to miss this view.

Her phone, which she'd locked in the glove compartment, buzzed. She fumbled with the latch and pulled it out in time to see a text message flash across the screen.

Denisha: I never did ask. Were you on your fifth year too?

Isabelle: Get your walking papers?

Denisha: Sure did. I could use a brainstorming buddy if you're available.

Isabelle: I'll start driving south.

Denisha: I'll head north.

Isabelle: Meet you in the middle?

Denisha: Meet you in the middle.

When Isabelle returned to Black Earth, she found Marilyn on the town hall steps, haloed by lamplight. Two duffle bags, a suitcase, and three boxes—all of Isabelle's worldly possessions—surrounded her. In her hands, Marilyn held a small package wrapped in brown paper and tied with twine.

Without a word, she handed it to Isabelle. Inside was the picture of the barefoot woman, cradling the basket, chin tilted resolutely for that journey up the river bluff. Now, when Isabelle studied the photograph, she noticed something new.

The woman wore the barest trace of a smile as well.

"Her fifth year," Isabelle said.

"Yes, indeed." Marilyn hugged her then, arms thin but capable. "We will miss you, but you are ready."

"And when it's time to come home?"

Marilyn raised her gaze to the river bluff. "You'll know, one way or the other."

On her way out of Black Earth, Isabelle passed a truck pulled over on the side of the road, a white pickup with flame decals. It sat there, discarded, forgotten, or most likely, both. A relic to something, although she wasn't quite sure what.

She drove into the night, listening to the whisper of wheels against the interstate and for the quiet murmur of her own heart.

Something is different in this part of the forest. Even the ground beneath Kit's feet feels unsubstantial to her sneakers. Like the solid earth might crumble away at any moment, and she would plunge into nothing.

Everything in her world feels like that right now—a slow and steady crumbling—all her plans, the heart that beats in her chest, even the lease on her studio apartment. Worst of all, her one bit of solace, the forest, spins around her, nothing solid and sure.

Except when she stumbles upon an old log. She's been here before, in this part of the forest, but how is it she's never seen this particular clearing, with this particular log?

The log is huge, reaching halfway up her thigh. The surface is rough even through her jeans, the bark baked warm by the sun.

Kit pulls out a thermos. Before her trek into the forest—ostensibly to think, but really, it was running away—she brewed hot cocoa. The real kind, in a pan on her two-burner stove. She measured out the cocoa and the sugar, adding a dash of vanilla and cinnamon.

Now she uncaps the thermos, and the aroma rides the crisp autumn air, filling it with rich chocolate and a hint of wood smoke. Kit inhales, and for that single moment, everything is okay.

Then the log beneath her rumbles. It's a rolling, tumbling, undulating motion that makes her think of a rollercoaster—and sends her plummeting backward and onto the ground.

She lands hard, breath leaving her in a whoosh, hot cocoa sloshing in the thermos. Somehow—*somehow*—she holds onto it, holds it steady and upright.

It's then she finds herself staring into a pair of huge amber eyes. They are the size of Kit's head—at least—and they glow with intensity. Beneath those eyes, she spies a snout and a pink, forked tongue.

She follows the elegant line of a neck to the large hump she earlier took for an old-growth log.

"You," she says now, testing her voice in the still air, "are a dragon, or I'm losing my mind."

The creature snorts, the scent of wood smoke with a hint of brimstone infusing the space around her.

"Although, I suppose there are worse ways to lose your mind."

The dragon snorts again as if in agreement.

"I'm Kit." She doesn't hold out her hand. One, she's still clutching the thermos. Two, she's not certain dragons shake hands.

The dragon bows its head in acknowledgment. Then, like a whisper, a word lights in Kit's mind.

Taggledorf.

"It's nice to meet you, Taggledorf."

The dragon thumps its tail once, and the earth shakes.

But this time, it doesn't feel as if the ground will crumble beneath her.

KIT VISITS THE SPOT OFTEN. Taggledorf doesn't always appear. Even when she—it's a long and complicated bit of pantomime to determine that Taggledorf is a she—doesn't, her presence is there. The air holds that scent of wood smoke. Sometimes there's brimstone.

But everything in that particular clearing grows a bit lusher, smells a bit richer. Hummingbirds flit and dragonflies buzz. In the winter, there is enough warmth radiating from Taggledorf's back that Kit can spend hours in the cold.

She brings the man she wants to make her husband to this spot. She does not expect Taggledorf to appear, but yes, it's a test. Her heart is still tender and cautious. While this man fills her with certainty, so did the other, the one that had her fleeing to the forest in the first place.

When she returns alone a week later and finds the clearing alive with forget-me-nots and wild roses, she has Taggledorf's answer.

She weaves a crown of roses for her friend, and when Taggledorf does appear, a bit shy, Kit places the wreath on the dragon's head.

"We will always be friends," she says.

SHE BRINGS her children to this spot, spreading a soft, flannel blanket across the clearing. In summer, they drink lemonade, in winter, hot cocoa. Taggledorf makes her scales shimmer and shine. The children spend hours slapping the scales with their chubby hands, squealing and shrieking with delight.

One time, the warm sunshine lulls Kit into a nap. She wakes, heart pounding and terrified, only to find that Taggledorf has corralled both children with her tail.

"Thank you, my friend." Kit sighs and leans into the old-growth that is and is not Taggledorf's midsection. "Thank you."

KIT DISCOVERS that Taggledorf loves stories. It's when she reads to her children that the dragon's scales glow and hum. Picture books and Mother Goose, eventually graduating to chapter books. Her children sit on the dragon's back and take turns reading aloud.

When they've moved on—to novels and textbooks and quantum mechanics—Kit takes to reading in the clearing any time she can. The heat against her back tells her which stories are her friend's favorites.

When her eyesight dims, and her hands no longer can hold an e-reader, never mind a paperback, she plays audiobooks for them.

In the sunshine, they rest, safe in the knowledge that nothing changes as long as the story goes on.

IT HAS BEEN months since Kit has visited the clearing, maybe even a year, but she doesn't want to think hard enough to count. Today is perfect for a trek—her last trek to her clearing.

The spring air is warm, but the path is still clear of summer growth, those brambles and branches that might trip her up.

Even so, the walk is long, much longer than when she pushed a double stroller along the dips and ruts. By the time she reaches the old-growth log that isn't a log, her legs nearly give out beneath her.

"No stories today, my friend. I only want to rest, with you." She sinks against her friend, knowing

Taggledorf will cushion her fall. "I have no wish to be found until ... after."

She snuggles against the dragon with the full knowledge that stories go on, but hers ends now.

And thanks to Taggledorf, it was a good one.

THE GIRL SMELLS FAMILIAR. This is the first thing Taggledorf notices. The second is the salt, so strong it has chapped the girl's cheeks and flavors the air.

Grief is something that can fill your mouth. This is something Taggledorf knows. It is something this girl is learning.

The girl settles next to her, back against Taggledorf's midsection, the very place where *she*—the other she—sat for so many years. The girl's body shakes, and Taggledorf lets the fire that always burns in her belly flare a bit—enough warmth to comfort and soothe while she ponders this girl.

She feels right.

Not everyone does, of course. That is the dragon's bane. So many of her kind have abandoned friendship, opting to gradually become the landscape they occupy.

But Taggledorf knows that despite the grief and goodbyes, a good friend is a story unto itself.

So she opens her large amber eyes and stares at the girl.

The gasp has more delight than fear.

The fingers are gentle against Taggledorf's snout.

"I miss her," the girl says.

Taggledorf nods. She does too.

"I'm Carly." The girl doesn't hold out her hand. She already knows that dragons don't shake hands.

Taggledorf blows a stream of smoke into the air. In it, is the sound of her name.

"It's nice to meet you," Carly says.

The dragon thumps her tail once, and the earth shakes.

And for now, at least, it doesn't feel as if the ground will crumble beneath either of them.

ABOUT THE AUTHOR

CHARITY TAHMASEB has slung corn on the cob for Green Giant and jumped out of airplanes (but not at the same time). She spent twelve years as a Girl Scout and six in the Army; that she wore a green uniform for both may not be a coincidence. These days, she writes fiction (long and short) and works as a technical writer for a software company in St. Paul.

Her short speculative fiction has appeared in *Flash Fiction Online*, *Deep Magic*, and *Cicada*.

ALSO BY CHARITY TAHMASEB

YOUNG ADULT FICTION (WITH DARCY VANCE)

The Geek Girl's Guide to Cheerleading

Dating on the Dork Side

YOUNG ADULT FICTION

The Fine Art of Keeping Quiet

The Fine Art of Holding Your Breath

Now and Later: Eight Young Adult Short Stories

PARANORMAL

Coffee and Ghosts, Season 1: Must Love Ghosts

Coffee and Ghosts, Season 2: The Ghost That Got Away

Coffee and Ghosts, Season 3: Nothing but the Ghosts

Coffee and Ghosts, Season 4: The Ghosts You Left Behind

FANTASY AND FAIRY TALES

Straying from the Path, Stories from the Sour Magic Series of Fairy Tales